Emma's Doll

VIKING/PUFFIN

Published by the Penguin Group
Penguin Books Ltd, 27 Wrights Lane, London W8 5TZ, England
Penguin Putnam Inc., 375 Hudson Street, New York, New York 10014, USA
Penguin Books Australia Ltd, Ringwood, Victoria, Australia
Penguin Books Canada Ltd, 10 Alcorn Avenue, Toronto, Ontario, Canada M4V 3B2
Penguin Books (NZ) Ltd, Private Bag 102902, NSMC, Auckland, New Zealand

Penguin Books Ltd, Registered Offices: Harmondsworth, Middlesex, England

First published by Viking 1998
1 3 5 7 9 10 8 6 4 2

Published in Puffin Books 1999
1 3 5 7 9 10 8 6 4 2

Printed in Hong Kong by Imago Publishing Limited

British Library Cataloguing in Publication Data
A CIP catalogue record for this book is available from the British Library

ISBN 0–670–87523–6 Hardback
ISBN 0–140–56245–1 Paperback

Emma's Doll

WRITTEN BY

Brian Patten

ILLUSTRATED BY

Alison Jay

VIKING

PUFFIN

WHEN

EMMA BROKE

her doll, her mother said,
"You will have to wait until
tomorrow to have her mended.
The Doll's Hospital is
closed tonight."

Emma nursed her doll,
but it grew paler and paler,
and when she went to bed that
night, Emma could not sleep.
She tossed and turned, and
her doll tossed and turned
beside her.

When her mother looked
into the room, Emma said,
"See how pale my doll is.
See how her head lolls and
her limbs dangle."
"Hush," said Emma's mother,
"try and sleep. Tomorrow
everything will be fine."

BUT EMMA COULD NOT SLEEP.
She went to her bedroom window and looked outside.
The world was frosty and white, and as cold as
her doll's cheeks.

"WE MUST MAKE YOU BETTER TONIGHT," SAID EMMA.
"Tomorrow is too far away and might never come."
And so Emma climbed down the stairs and
went out into the night.

EMMA FOUND HERSELF

in an enchanted wood. She looked up into the branches and
asked the owls if they could help her doll, but all they did was
blink and hoot and shake their heads.

A SHADOW DETACHED
itself from among the leaves. It was a jay.
"Give me the doll," it said. "I will nurse it here
among the swaying branches. Give it me."
"No," said Emma. "You will hoard her away in
your nest and I'll not see her again."

FROM AMONG THE
branches of another tree flew a dove.
It glowed in the darkness. "Don't listen to the jay,"
it said. "Let me help you."

THE DOVE GUIDED

Emma through the dark wood and led her to a
path beside which a small dragon lay curled up fast asleep.
Its breath was so warm it had melted the frost,
and tiny flowers grew all around it.

EMMA LOOKED DOWN

the path. "Is this the right path?" she asked.
"It is the only path," said the dove. "You have no
choice but to follow it."

EMMA

SET OFF
down the solitary
path through the wood.
Soon she came to a
clearing in which she saw a
merry-go-round, and on
it six dwarfs sat astride
wooden horses.
"Can any of you help my
doll?" Emma asked the
dwarfs. "Her cheeks are
cold and as white
as the frost."
But the dwarfs paid
no attention to Emma.
They laughed and rocked
about in their saddles and
sang, and they were so
noisy that their singing
drowned out Emma's
voice and they did
not hear her.

EMMA WALKED DEEPER
and deeper into the wood, far from her
mother's house, and she met a witch who said,
"Let me cradle your doll. I will nurse it."
"No," said Emma. "Witches' arms were not meant for nursing
dolls. They are arms of frost and brambles. Go away."

THE WITCH FLED

through the trees complaining,
"I have nursed seeds locked in the frozen earth.
I have nursed the waning moon.
A doll is no different."

"SURELY THERE IS
someone in the wood I can trust to mend you,"
Emma said to her doll.
"What a silly child," said a voice. "What a very silly child to be
talking to a doll. It is no use to you. Give it here."
Emma saw a wolf. Its coat was made of velvet rags and
between its paws it held a sack full of objects it had gathered
at random from the wood.

"MY CHILDREN NEED
such a thing," it said. "Give it to me."
"No," said Emma. "Your children would tear her dress,
and sharpen their teeth on her arms."
The wolf snarled at Emma, and it would have pounced on her,
but a vast roar shook the wood and frightened it away.

A

GOLDEN LION APPEARED
from among the trees and
knelt down in front of
Emma.

Its thick mane smelt as
sweet and fresh as her
mother's hair. Emma and
her doll snuggled into the
lion's mane and rode away
on its back.

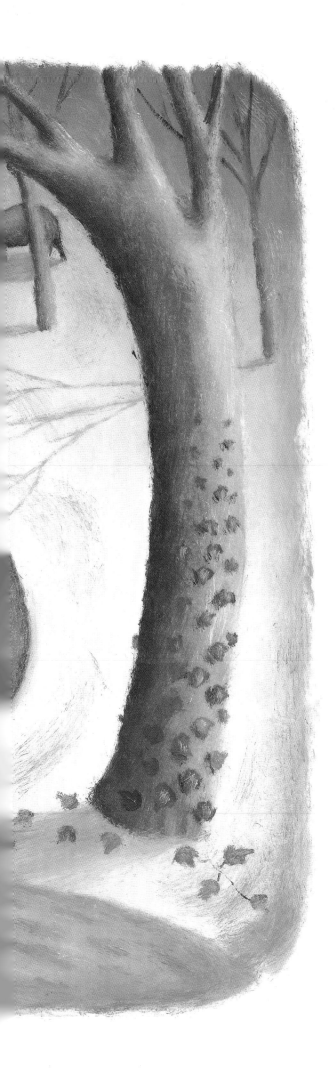

THEY CAME TO
a glade in the wood, where
a badger and a hare lay
sleeping beside a pool.

Emma climbed
down from the lion and sat
between them, clutching her
doll tightly. She fell asleep, and
the lion padded softly away,
knowing she was safe.

When Emma woke, the badger
and the hare had gone. Her
doll had also gone. It was
nowhere to be seen.

EMMA SEARCHED FOR her doll among the bushes and the tangled undergrowth. She peered down warrens and among the roots of trees, and then, in the very centre of the enchanted wood, she found her doll again.

She was being fed from a large silver spoon by a hippopotamus. The dragon, the lion, the hare, the badger, and the dove stood watching.

"What are you feeding my doll?" asked Emma.
"The medicine of dreams," said the hippopotamus.

It was the best medicine her doll could have, for she opened her eyes and smiled at Emma.

"I no longer feel cold," she said.
"I am better now."

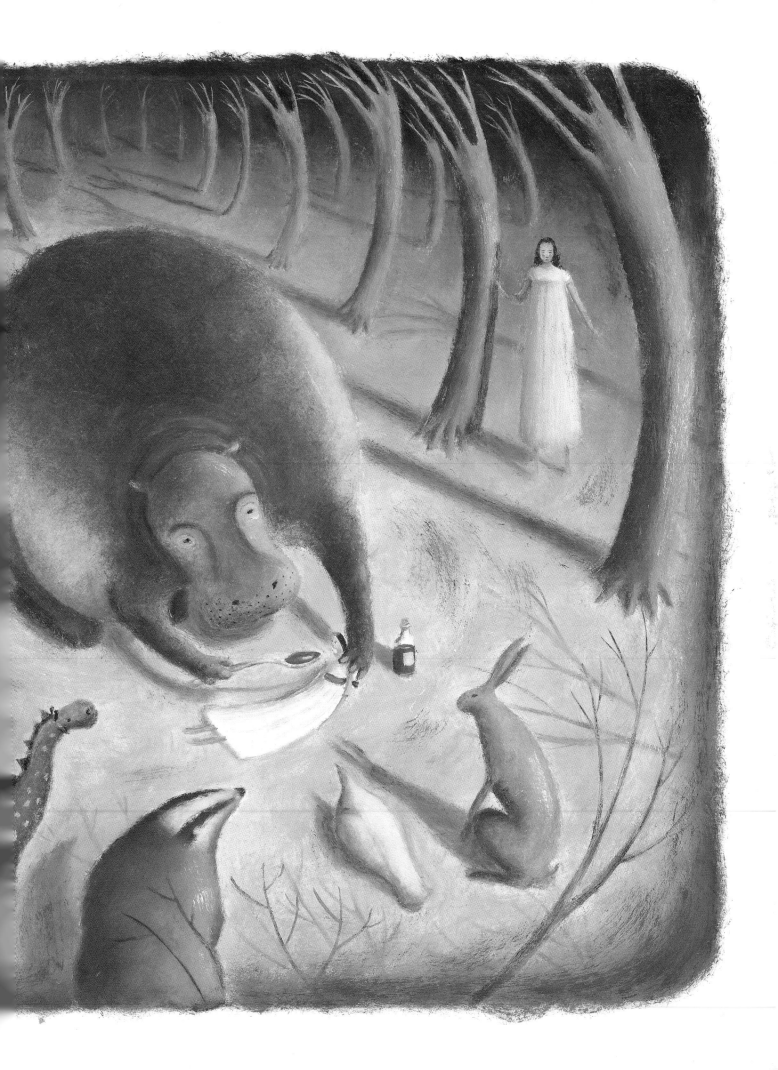

EMMA LED HER
doll back home through the wood.
The dwarfs and their merry-go-round
had vanished. The dragon was no longer
beside the path. There was no sign of the
witch or the wolf. The jay had flown off
into the fields, and the owls
were falling asleep.

EMMA AND HER
doll left the enchanted
wood. They climbed quietly
back upstairs into their bedroom.
Emma fell asleep, and her
doll slept warm and safe
beside her.